I Can Read

ALVIN
AND
THE CHIPMUNKS

CHIPWRECKED

TOO COOL FOR RULES

ADAPTED BY J. E. BRIGHT

HARPER

An Imprint of HarperCollinsPublishers

The Chipmunks and The Chipettes
were going on a vacation cruise!
They all were excited,
but no one was more excited than Alvin.

Alvin wanted to have fun.

He wanted to go parasailing,

but Dave said he was too young.

"We'll have fun as a family,"

said Dave, "but with some rules."

"Don't worry," replied Alvin.

"Rules is my middle name!"

But Alvin wasted no time getting into trouble.

He squirted sunscreen on the deck, causing Dave to slip.

Simon and Theodore were worried.
They thought Alvin was going to get
them all in trouble—again.

The trip had barely begun.
Dave was already yelling
at Alvin.

Before bed, Dave reminded Alvin

that he had promised to follow the rules.

The chipmunks had to stay

in their room while Dave

had dinner with the ship's captain.

Alvin promised to behave.

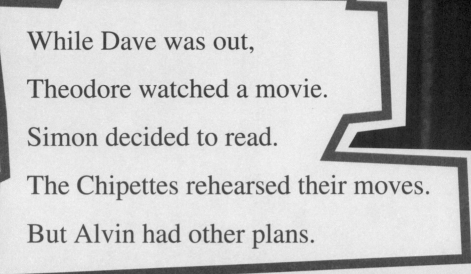

While Dave was out,

Theodore watched a movie.

Simon decided to read.

The Chipettes rehearsed their moves.

But Alvin had other plans.

He put on a tuxedo and

went to the casino!

13

Simon followed Alvin to the casino.

He tried to stop Alvin,

but Alvin just wanted to have fun!

Alvin even met a girl.

"I'm not that young," he said.

"I'm in a casino way past my bedtime!

No one tells me what to do."

Dave found Alvin and Simon and
dragged them out of the casino.
"You are in a lot of trouble!"
hollered Dave.
"Do we have to walk the plank?"
asked Alvin.
"There's no plank," replied Dave,
"but if you disobey me again,
we will be kicked off the ship!"

The next day, Dave took a nap

while the Chipmunks played shuffleboard.

It wasn't much fun.

"It's ten percent shuffle and

ninety percent bored," Simon said.

Then, Alvin had an idea.

He borrowed a boy's kite,

but the wind was too strong!

The Chipmunks and The Chipettes

tried to help, but instead, they all

soared into the sky!

19

The Chipmunks and The Chipettes

flew over the ocean

and landed on a tiny island.

Stranded on the island,

they waited to be rescued.

Without Dave to help,

even Alvin was worried.

That night, Simon built a fire,

but Theodore put it out by mistake.

They all slept through a cold night.

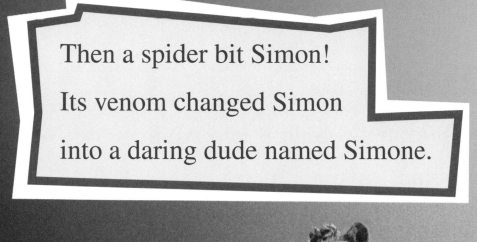

Then a spider bit Simon!
Its venom changed Simon
into a daring dude named Simone.

Simone wouldn't help Alvin

collect wood to build a shelter.

He danced in the rain instead.

Alvin tried to get Simone

to stop doing dangerous things.

"Careful!" cried Alvin.

"You could get hurt! SIIIMOONN!"

"You sound like Dave," said Brittany.

If Alvin couldn't be the fun one,

He would be the responsible one.

He and Brittany built an amazing shelter.

"I know why Dave hasn't come,"
said Alvin. "He's not looking."
"Why wouldn't he?" asked Brittany.
"I drive him crazy," Alvin said.
What Alvin didn't know was that
Dave was on his way!

Then the island's volcano rumbled and released hot smoke.

"That's why the water here is so hot. It's being heated by an underground magma chamber!" Brittany said.

"How did you know that?" Jeanette asked.

"The place where I get my nails done always has the science channel on," Brittany said.

Alvin was giving everyone orders

to get them all safely off the island.

Out of the jungle, Dave appeared.

"What can I do to help?" asked Dave.

Alvin burst into tears.

"I thought you weren't looking for us

because I'm such a pain," Alvin cried.

"You are a pain," replied Dave.

"But I'd come no matter what."

31

They escaped the island
just as the volcano erupted.
"I want to say I'm sorry
for ruining our vacation,"
Alvin said.
Dave smiled, impressed,
and pointed at the helicopter above.

I Can Read Book® is a trademark of HarperCollins Publishers.

Alvin and the Chipmunks: Chipwrecked © 2011 Twentieth Century Fox Film Corporation and Regency Entertainment (USA), Inc. in the U.S. only. © 2011 Twentieth Century Fox Film Corporation and Monarchy Enterprises S.a.r.l. in all other territories. Alvin and the Chipmunks, The Chipettes, and Characters TM & © 2011 Bagdasarian Productions, LLC. All rights reserved.
Printed in the United States of America.
No part of this book may be used or reproduced in any manner whatsoever without written permission except in the case of brief quotations embodied in critical articles and reviews. For information address HarperCollins Children's Books, a division of HarperCollins Publishers, 10 East 53rd Street, New York, NY 10022.
www.icanread.com

Library of Congress catalog card number: 2011933989
ISBN 978-0-06-208602-0

11 12 13 14 15 LP/WOR 10 9 8 7 6 5 4 3 2 1   ❖   First Edition

Dear Parent:
Your child's love of reading starts here!

Every child learns to read in a different way and at his or her own speed. Some go back and forth between reading levels and read favorite books again and again. Others read through each level in order. You can help your young reader improve and become more confident by encouraging his or her own interests and abilities. From books your child reads with you to the first books he or she reads alone, there are I Can Read Books for every stage of reading:

SHARED READING
Basic language, word repetition, and whimsical illustrations, ideal for sharing with your emergent reader

BEGINNING READING
Short sentences, familiar words, and simple concepts for children eager to read on their own

READING WITH HELP
Engaging stories, longer sentences, and language play for developing readers

READING ALONE
Complex plots, challenging vocabulary, and high-interest topics for the independent reader

ADVANCED READING
Short paragraphs, chapters, and exciting themes for the perfect bridge to chapter books

I Can Read Books have introduced children to the joy of reading since 1957. Featuring award-winning authors and illustrators and a fabulous cast of beloved characters, I Can Read Books set the standard for beginning readers.

A lifetime of discovery begins with the magical words **"I Can Read!"**

Visit www.icanread.com for information
on enriching your child's reading experience.